Cover design by CirceCorp

99designs.ca/profiles/circecorpdesign

ISBN: 978-0-9953281-3-6

Cheshire Books

For Sam and Dean Winchester –
Because people are the greatest monsters of all.

CRAZIES

JAY ALLISAN

HE WOKE from a dead sleep in the middle of the night to the absence in his bed. The room was too dark to see even the few inches to his left, to see the vacant pillow or the blankets thrown back in a heap, but he felt them, first with his gut and then with his hand. He patted the mattress and his hand came back damp, and now he could smell it, the sharp scent of ammonia, and he shook the urine off his hand and wrinkled his nose and swore under his breath and wiped his hand on the sheets. He got out of bed.

The room was so dark he couldn't make out a thing. The door was closed. The blackout shades were drawn. He took two steps forward and extended his hand. It landed precisely on the light switch. He knew where everything in the room was, could picture it in his mind, could *feel* it, the same way he could feel she was no longer in the room. He flicked on the light switch anyhow, to check. The naked bulb on the ceiling cast the room in a yellowish glow. The door behind him, leading to the bathroom, was shut. The door to his right, the walk-in closet, shut. The bed pushed up against the wall, empty. The window with the shades drawn. The dresser with alternating his-and-hers drawers. His night table. Her writing desk with its clunky blue typewriter.

She wasn't there.

He checked the bathroom first, which was logical. He checked the closet next, which was also logical. He stripped the soiled sheets off the bed and opened the bedroom door, which moved silently on its hinges. He frowned. He'd always heard her get up before. She'd never left the bedroom without him knowing. He had no idea how long it had been since she'd woken. He hurried to the laundry closet across the hall, threw the bedding in the washer but didn't start the machine, turned the light off in the bedroom, closed the door, and descended the staircase quietly. Listening.

No lights were on, but the lower levels of the house weren't quite as black as the upstairs. Here the shades were the regular kind, the slatted kind that filtered the outside light but didn't kill it, that looked like gray squares with silver halos where the shades didn't quite meet the window frame. Here he could see angles, shadows, shapes in the darkness. At the bottom of the stairs, to the left, he could see through the opening to the kitchen. The small window above the sink made the faucet gleam. The refrigerator hummed. He could hear the steady *tik-tok* of the clock.

To the right was the entryway, with its little wooden pony wall separating it from the living room. Yellow streetlight poured in through the window above the front

2

door. A sudden fear she'd gone outside had him jumping to the landing from four stairs up, landing with a thump he barely registered over the pounding of his heart. He took hold the doorknob and gave it a twist. Still locked. So was the deadbolt. He crossed straight into the kitchen, to check the back door. Also locked. He let out a sigh and pushed his hand through his hair, and his heart began to settle.

The back door was in the small dining alcove, and above the old round table hung the clock. Here the *tik-tok* was louder. It was one of those old cartoon clocks, a black and white cat, with a swinging pendulum for a tail and eyes that went back and forth. He glanced at it briefly on his way into the living room. Half past one in the morning.

He looked now at the shadows and shapes in the living room. The television in its media cabinet, situated in the corner. The fireplace to its left. Two chairs, two side tables, and a couch arranged in a semi-circle around the coffee table. Two table lamps and a floor lamp. The cat bed beside the couch.

And there, on the floor, wedged tight between the couch and a side table, a white so bright it was almost luminescent, curled up, trembling, rocking back and forth, emitting a high, keening hum that came and went with the wracking of her shoulders, was she.

He went to her.

"Hah-*hmmmm*… hah-*hmmmm*…"

The sound grew louder as he approached. Gaspy at the start and manic at the finish. She was balanced on the balls of her feet, her knees tucked up to her chest. Her hands were pressed over her ears.

3

"Honey?"

"Hah-*hmmmm…*"

She rocked. He knelt in front of her.

"Honey."

"Hah-*hmmmm…*"

She smelled of urine. He put his hands gently over hers.

"Hah-*aaaaaahh—*"

"Don't scream," he said, and drew her hands away from her ears. "It's just me," he said, and lifted her face to meet his. Eyes wide and white as dinner plates skittered wildly around the room before settling on him. She blinked, doll-like, her eyelids shuttering up and down. Her head drooped, and in the gray darkness her cheeks gleamed with tears.

"It's all right," he said, as her shoulders shook. "It's all right. I'm here."

She cried, but quietly, not making a sound. He waited until the tears and the trembling had stopped. He said it again.

"I'm here."

Holding firmly to her hands, he stood, lifting her to her feet. Her white nightgown billowed around her like a parachute unfolding. Her skin was clammy and prickled with gooseflesh beneath his touch.

"I didn't hear you get up," he said, as he led her to the stairs. She trailed one step behind him, one arm limp at her side, the other outstretched, caught in his grasp. Her dark hair hung in a curtain, obscuring her bowed head. The carpet swallowed their footfalls.

He asked, "Why didn't you wake me?"

He listened, but there was no response.

When they reached the bedroom he turned on the light. He sat her at her writing desk while he put fresh sheets on the bed. When he'd finished he brought her into the bathroom. He pulled the white nightgown over her head and left her standing there while he brought it to the washer. She hadn't moved when he returned.

He took a warm washcloth and soaped her from breasts to thighs. He washed her until the stench of urine was gone. He held her hands beneath the tap and washed them too. He brought her back into the bedroom and guided a clean white nightgown over her head. He settled her in bed.

"Was it a dream?" he asked, as he sat on the edge of the bed. She was reclined on the pillows he'd propped up against the brass headboard. Her legs stretched out beneath the sheets in two parallel lines, her hands in her lap, palm-up. Her mouth was slack. Her eyes were vacant.

He waited, and at last she spoke.

"A bad dream," she whispered, almost too quiet for him to hear. "It was a bad dream."

"I'll make you some tea."

He pressed his lips to the crown of her head and started toward the stairs. He stopped in the doorway and glanced back. She was staring at the dim yellow lightbulb on the ceiling. Her lips moved. He couldn't hear her. But he heard her all the same.

They're watching me.

He drew the door closed behind him. It moved silently on its hinges. He descended the stairs to the kitchen to make the tea. He listened to the clock *tik-tok* while he waited.

5

IN THE morning he let her sleep in, because he didn't have to work. She lay on her side, her back to him. He moved closer to her and put his arm around her waist. She sighed in her sleep. He breathed in the vanilla scent of her shampoo. The room was dark, with its blackout shades drawn and the door shut tight. The house was quiet. The world was still.

He held her safe against his chest, and they slept.

BY THE time they got up it was late in the morning. The blackout shades could no longer keep the daylight at bay. In the hall he could hear meowing, and pitiful scratching on the door. He smoothed back her hair and kissed her temple.

"Time to get up. Your cat needs you."

He showered, slowly, lingering in the warm water and

thick steam. He could smell breakfast when he emerged. Pancakes. Eggs. The usual weekend fare. He remembered the first time she'd made him breakfast and felt pride at how far she'd come.

All the blinds remained drawn downstairs, but plenty of light came in anyway. No need to turn on a lamp. The table was heavy with plates piled high. She was still at the stove, frying the last of the eggs, tossing pieces down to the cat. She licked grease off her fingers and glanced up at him. Her smile was shy, her cheeks faintly rosy. He went to her and kissed her until the eggs were burned. He turned off the stove and kissed her some more.

After breakfast they cleaned up the dishes together. He washed, she dried. She put them away. He made her a cup of tea and they retired to the living room.

It was Saturday. They had a routine. First they would work on a puzzle. The current one was so large it nearly overflowed the coffee table. They had the corners and the edges, and a couple spots that hung down like stalactites. They'd started it last week. He expected they'd be finished it by next.

After the puzzle came music. Sometimes they just sat together and listened, and sometimes they would dance. He had quite the collection of records, everything from Bach to the Bee Gees. He would let her pick the album. Sometimes she would pick two.

When they'd had enough of music they would play a game. The left side of the media cabinet was filled with games. Card games, board games, checkers, chess. She was competitive. They could play for hours.

By the time she'd tired of the games it would be early evening. He would read a novel while she prepared supper, and when supper was done they would watch a movie. Rows and rows of DVDs filled the right side of the media cabinet. She would open the cabinet door and run her finger over the boxes, smiling at her favorites, turning to ask him *what about this?* He was happy to watch whatever she wanted. He would sit on the couch and she would curl up beside him, and sometimes the cat would curl up beside her, and they would finish out the day in comfortable silence, in the darkness of the living room, in the company of Mary Poppins or Willy Wonka.

It was Saturday, and they had a routine. So when they retired to the living room and sat cross-legged on the floor in front of the coffee table, he began picking through the puzzle pieces without noticing something was wrong. She was quiet, but she often was. She seemed distracted, but that wasn't unusual. It was only when he gave a cry of joy after matching a piece that he looked up from the puzzle and saw what she was doing. Where she was looking.

At the window.

At the door.

She was biting her thumbnail and looking at the door.

"Honey."

Her gaze didn't come back to him. Her teeth worked viciously at the tender skin around her thumbnail. He saw blood bead on her skin. He snatched her hand away from her mouth and held it firmly in both of his.

"Look at me."

She was trembling. He gripped her hand tighter.

8

"*Look at me.*"

He didn't shout. He never shouted. But it was a command. And she obeyed.

"We're doing a puzzle," he said, gentler now. "You like the puzzles. Don't you?"

She nodded meekly.

"Say it."

"I like the puzzles."

"Then let's focus on the puzzle."

But first he had to tend to her hand. There was a first aid kit above the fridge, so he brought her into the kitchen and held her hand beneath the tap until the blood was washed away. He applied ointment to the raw skin and wrapped the thumb in a bandage. He lifted her hand to his mouth and kissed it.

"You should be more careful," he told her. "Say it."

"I should be more careful."

"You don't want to hurt yourself."

"I don't want to hurt myself."

"Do you want to do the puzzle?"

"Do I want to do the puzzle?"

He smiled fondly and kissed her hand again. "I'm asking. We can do something else if you want."

He waited, watching how she watched him uncertainly. Her dark hair had not been brushed today. It hung like a curtain, half-obscuring her face. It hid the curves of her cheeks, soft and pale as floured dough. It hid the delicate column of her neck. It did not hide her eyes, which flickered like obsidian flames, going right-left, right-left, unable to hold his gaze.

She whispered, "No. I like the puzzles."

"Good," he said. "Then that's what we'll do. But first, maybe you'd like some more tea."

He put the kettle on and they returned to the living room. It was Saturday, after all. They had a routine.

SHE DID not want to go to bed that night.

The rest of the day had been fine. They finished half the puzzle, listened to ZZ Top, played Boggle and Mouse Trap and watched *The Jungle Book* after dinner. She'd drowsed on his shoulder, one hand absently stroking the cat. She was calm. Relaxed. Docile. But as soon as he turned the television off and put the DVD away, she came awake like a live wire.

She curled into the corner of the couch and pulled her knees to her chest. He held out his hand.

"Come on, now. It's time for bed."

She shook her head.

"It's nearly 10. You'll be tired tomorrow if you don't get to bed soon."

"I don't want to," she whispered.

He returned to the couch and sat across from her. She curled smaller. He took her hands gently.

"What is it? What are you afraid of?"

She pressed her lips together in a quivering line. Her hands were cold. Tears threatened in her eyes.

"They'll watch me," she whispered.

"No one will watch you."

"They're always watching me."

"Who is?"

"The lamps."

He was too startled to form a response. Her fear of being watched was a long-running one, but never before had the ubiquitous *they* been identified. *They* were in the abstract. *They* were a product of her mind.

"Honey," he said, "why would the lamps be watching you?"

"Because they have eyes."

She was staring at the lamps now, as if in a show of defiance. As if letting them know she was onto them. He glanced at the lamps himself. There were three in the living room, two table and one floor. All were simple, no strange colors or complex patterns. Nothing about them suggested eyes.

"Show me where the eyes are," he said. He rose from the couch and waited for her to follow.

She did follow, hesitantly, wary of turning her back on any of the lamps. She went to the nearest one, a table lamp, shaped like a vase and the color of young pine trees. She did not touch the lamp or even look at it. Instead she followed its cord.

"There," she said, pointing a trembling finger at the wall socket. "It's looking. It's looking at me."

He tilted his head and squinted, and he supposed if you were looking for it, the outlet did somewhat resemble a pair of eyes. Two vertical slits, with a small round hole that could be a mouth or a nose. But that was the bottom half of the outlet, where nothing was plugged in. The top eyes were obscured because of the lamp.

He could have asked her how the outlet could see if it had two prongs buried deep in its eyes. He should have asked her what the outlet's eyes had to do with the lamp being able to see. Many other things in the house were plugged in. Could the oven see? Or the refrigerator? Or the vacuum? Why would the lamps be watching her while she slept, if they were turned off? How could the living room lamps see her all the way upstairs? There were no lamps in the bedroom. Just the single naked bulb on the ceiling with no outlet in sight.

He should have listened to her fears and explained them away, and if explanations failed, he should have comforted her. He did none of these things. He was startled and angry and maybe a little afraid.

Because she thought the lamps were watching her.

"Suit yourself then," he said, and switched off the lights and left her alone in the living room while he went upstairs by himself. He heard her whimper of fear but did not turn back. He washed his face and brushed his teeth, then undressed and climbed into bed. He waited.

It did not take long. He'd closed the door behind him, and while he didn't hear it open, he heard her soft footfalls on the carpet when she entered the room. He heard the creak of the bed as she crept in on the other side. He heard her muffled gasps as she sobbed quietly into her pillow.

He should have said something to her, some kind words that would bring her comfort. He should have reached out to her, held her, to show her she was safe. He did none of these things. He just let her cry until she fell asleep.

He lay awake for a good while after that, thinking. About

the day. The nail biting and the blood. The lamps and the eyes. Something was changing.

He would not let it. He would stop it. He would fix it. For her.

She had always been worth saving.

O N SUNDAY he was the one who disrupted their routine.

Weekends were their time together, hard-fought time he cherished above all. He enjoyed his job. He worked hard at his job. But his job was demanding, and it consumed five days a week. Weekends were the reason he worked as he did. Weekends were the prize for sixty hours apart. And after all their years together, weekends were finally the way he'd always hoped. Just the two of them, happy to be together. Shared affection. Mutual companionship.

He would not let that slip away.

So on Sunday morning he roused her roughly, with a hard shake to the shoulders.

"Get up," he said. "You've got work to do."

Something passed across her face, a flicker of hesitancy,

disbelief. Then she understood. She hurried out of bed and went down the stairs, and soon he heard the clanging of pots and pans. She'd be preparing him breakfast again, even though on Sunday it was his turn to cook.

He listened for a moment more, then got into the shower. There was no lingering today. He was out in minutes, and after giving his hair a brisk rub with the towel, he dressed and started downstairs. He paused halfway down the steps, then turned around. He went into the bedroom closet. Deep in the back, hidden beneath the insole of one of his shoes, was a key on a leather cord. He put it around his neck and left it hanging outside his shirt. He descended to the kitchen.

She was rushing, trying to crack eggs and butter toast and slice oranges all at once. He made no move to help her. He stood watching, not in her way but where she couldn't miss him, and she rushed all the faster. Until she saw what was around his neck. That made her stop, and drop the carton of milk in her hand. It splashed all over the kitchen floor.

She grabbed a swath of paper towel and fell to her knees, whispering, "I'm sorry, I'm sorry, I'll clean it up…"

"Yes you will." He stood there and watched her do it.

When she'd finished the toast was burned. The eggs had to be scraped from the pan. The oranges were a hacked-up mess, so he threw them in the trash. He sat down at the table and made her eat the rest.

She did the dishes in silence afterward, alone, while he watched. Already she was cowed. He could see it in the way her shoulders slumped, in the way she ducked her head. He

15

did not like to see her this way, but he knew that after yesterday it was necessary. Perhaps if he'd been more firm with her, yesterday wouldn't have happened at all. It was his fault. He'd gotten too comfortable, too complacent. Now he had to regain control before it was lost.

The blinds were shut. The lights were off. Yet the whole main floor was lit with a golden glow, from the brilliant day outside that wouldn't be denied. It had been too long since he'd aired the place out. Today was as good a day as any. Especially given the circumstances.

"What are you going to do today?" he asked her, as a test. To see if she understood. If she answered *crafts*, or *read a book*, or any of the other usual Sunday activities, he'd have to take things further. But if she understood then he would reward her, and they could slowly return to normal.

She was still at the sink, elbow-deep in suds. She didn't look up.

"Chores," she said quietly. "Got to clean the place up."

He nodded in approval. That was the answer he'd hoped for. He let her finish the dishes, and when she was done he went to her and took hold of her hands. He stroked his thumb tenderly over her bandaged one.

"You need a new bandage," he said. "Let me change it."

She held perfectly still as he removed the old bandage and applied ointment and a fresh one. The wound was small and had long since stopped bleeding. For anyone else a new bandage would be overkill. For her it was a necessity. He'd like to see her further cover it with a pair of gloves, which made cleaning the perfect task for yet another reason.

He smoothed back a mass of her unruly dark hair. She

stiffened at the touch, then relaxed as he let his hand trail down her cheek and come to rest beneath her chin. He tipped her face up and was pleased to see the look in her eyes had shifted from fear to trust, from resignation to hope. It was a delicate balance, a game of give and take. He would give her the comfort she needed in the end, but, as much as he may have wished otherwise, he wasn't finished taking yet.

"Clean upstairs today," he told her. "It's time I aired these rooms out."

He watched her, and though all she did was nod, he could see how he had crushed her. It was a banishment, pure and simple. A blatant rejection. And still he wasn't finished.

He withdrew his hand from beneath her chin and sharpened his tone. "If that's a problem, you could always go down—"

He didn't even have to say it. Her eyes had gone wide and she answered before he could finish.

"I'll clean upstairs. Of course. I'll clean upstairs."

"Good," he said. Her dark eyes were glued to the key around his neck and her face had lost all hint of color. The feeling it gave him was not pleasure, but it was certainly akin to satisfaction. He'd done what he needed to. It was for her own good.

"You understand," he said, and she nodded fervently. "Go on, then. And wear gloves!" he called after her as she bolted from the room.

HE STOOD in the kitchen in front of the sink, the cord to the blinds in his hands. He held it with reverence, enjoying the anticipation. Then he gave it a hard tug.

The kitchen lit up with brilliance, the unobstructed sunshine so bright he had to shield his eyes. He went to the back door and opened those blinds as well. The small dining alcove went from dusk to high noon in an instant.

He abandoned the dining alcove for the living room, chasing away the gloomy shadows as he opened the blinds there one by one, until every window was uncovered, until no darkness remained. He looked around the room and found it almost unfamiliar in the natural light.

Now for a little fresh air.

It was early spring, but the days had been mild and the air had been crisp, and the house was admittedly stale. He went to the left-hand window of the bank of three and turned the crank. It was sticky at first, from the winter or from disuse, but slowly it turned, and slowly the window pushed open. A cool breeze ruffled his hair and he smiled. He went into the kitchen.

He took hold of the crank on the window above the sink, and this one required a little extra elbow grease. He leaned on it heavily, and the window pushed out, and the brisk air tingled on his skin. He stood there in front of the window, letting the air refresh him, listening to the air flow from the back of the house to the front, imagining it rustling through the carpet, permeating the furniture, carrying out all the pent-up must until the indoors smelled like the outdoors. He entered the dining alcove and opened the back door.

And now the breeze hit him, really hit him from head to toe, as he held open the main door and let the wind funnel in through the screen door. He looked out onto his back deck.

As fresh and bright as the house was becoming with all the new air and new light flooding in, it wasn't enough, not for him. Not today. Maybe it was yesterday's nail-biting and fixation on lamps, maybe it was today's necessitated repercussions, but he didn't want to be in the house right now, especially since he wouldn't be spending that time with her. She would be cleaning upstairs for the foreseeable future, and what else would he do in the meantime? The outside was calling to him.

He heeded the call and stepped out onto his deck.

He looked around, then closed his eyes to enjoy the moment if only for a moment, because good God, the yard was a disaster. He hadn't done much fall cleanup and winter had taken its toll. Clumps of leaves overflowed the roof gutters, half the branches on the tree were dead, and garbage had either been blown across the yard or dragged across the yard by some neighborhood creature. There were still a few spots of melting snow in the shade of the tree, but otherwise the ground was bare, the patchy brown grass looking prickly and uneven. The fence needed painting. The shrubs were overgrown.

"Ahoy!"

The voice came out of nowhere, startling him, and he clutched at the deck railing as his eyes flew open and he lost his balance. The deck railing bowed beneath his grip, and he cursed twice in quick succession. The first curse was for the railing, which was rotting and would need to be replaced. The second was for the realization that Lou was out in his yard next door and had spotted him. Snoopy Lou, his longtime neighbor, who took a keener interest in him than he'd have liked. They'd chatted on Friday, a quick exchange about the weather as they'd pulled into their respective driveways. It was about as much conversation as he cared to have, but ignoring Lou would be rude. He let go of the deck railing and gave Lou a wave.

"Morning, Lou!" he called cheerfully. "Beautiful day today, isn't it?"

"Oh, a real beaut today, she is. A real beaut."

Lou abandoned the pile of leaves he was raking and came over to their shared fence, resting his arms atop the fence and his chin on his arms. Lou meant to talk awhile. With a sense of reluctance he descended the deck stairs and met Lou at the fence. He nodded at Lou's pile of leaves.

"Getting a head start on the spring cleanup?"

Lou scratched his chin and gave a ragged smile. "Ah, just needed something to do out here. Can't stay inside on a day like this. Good timing for you, eh? Didn't have to be at the clinic today?"

"No," he said. "I try to take weekends off."

"Do ya? Boy, that's nice. Guess that's the idea though, ain't it? Private practice, I mean. Sure beats a hospital, am I right? Get some downtime for yourself."

He nodded agreeably. Lou squinted into the brilliant sun.

"Must keep you busy, though," Lou said. "It's been what, ten years since the hospital burned down? And there's still nothing in the works yet to replace it. That's gotta put the pressure on guys like you, keeping all the crazies in check. Seems like you can't turn around anymore without hearing about some psycho going off his meds and murdering his family. Good thing we got guys like you holding the line."

"I do my best," he said. It was his customary response to a tired rhetoric.

"Too bad you ain't a real doctor, though," Lou said, and guffawed. "My Martha's arthritis is acting up again. Ankles the size of cantaloupes. She can barely get down the stairs, and the doc that's treating her now can't do a damn thing. Nothing worse than watching the love of your life suffer like that. It makes a man desperate. You know what I mean?"

"I do," he said, and thought it was the most honest thing he'd ever said to Snoopy Lou.

Lou gave him a sheepish smile. "Yeah, I guess you would now, wouldn't you? That's your life's work, as they say. Forgive an old man. You get sentimental at my age. Heck, next thing you know I'll be in to see you!"

"Take your time," he said. "I'm booked for weeks."

Lou hooted with laughter. "Damn right you are! Damn crazies." Lou pushed away from the fence. "I suppose I'd better let you go. Last thing you want is to be stuck jawing with an old coot when you're supposed to be having time off. You'll never meet any young ladies that way, nice or otherwise. You gotta mix a little play in with all that work, am I right?"

He rolled his eyes good-naturedly. Lou shook a finger at him.

"Next time I see you there'd better be a ring on your finger, or at least a pair of panties in your pocket. Take my advice, young fella. No man makes it in this world alone."

"I'll do my best," he said again. It was his customary

response to a tired rhetoric.

Lou cast a glance toward his house. "I'd best run in, check on Martha. I'll be seeing you, doc. Don't forget about what I said!"

"You'll only say it again," he muttered under his breath, as he watched Lou head back inside. He really ought to get a ring. But then Lou would want to meet the lucky lady, and that wouldn't do. Better to stay the course and play the bachelor.

He turned toward his own house, intent on taking a better look at that rotted deck railing. But movement from above him caught his eye. If he'd looked a second later he might have missed it, but somehow he'd timed it perfectly. He saw the face pressed to the window and its quick disappearance. He saw the unfurling of the blackout shades as they dropped back to the sill.

He went inside the house.

THE VACUUM was running. He closed the back door behind him and drew the blinds. He closed the window above the sink and drew the blinds. He closed the window in the living room and drew the blinds. When the house was all shut up again he started up the stairs.

The noise of the vacuum grew louder as he approached. She was vacuuming the bedroom but had plugged the machine in in the hall. He pulled the plug out of the wall and the noise went away. He went into the bedroom.

She was still pushing the vacuum, bumping it up against the baseboards, dragging it fruitlessly back and forth. The shades were drawn, the room bathed in the dim yellow light from the bare bulb on the ceiling. Her head was down, watching the vacuum. Its wheels made parallel tracks on the carpet.

"Stop," he said. "It's off."

She kept vacuuming. He took hold of her wrist and she stilled. Her head stayed bowed.

"Got to clean," she whispered. "Got to clean the place up. I'm doing chores, I'm doing my chores. Got to clean the place up."

He felt her pulse hammering in the wrist he held. He asked, "Were you cleaning the window?"

Her pulse raced. "No. No. I don't clean the window. The windows don't need to be cleaned."

"Look at me."

She was trembling all over, quivering, swaying, so unsteady she may have collapsed if not for his grip on her wrist. He waited, and slowly she raised her chin, bit by bit, until she was looking at him, and her mouth was trembling too, and her eyes were wide and fearful and her cheeks were wet with tears. He laid his hand on her cheek and she closed her eyes, trembling. He brushed away the tears. He tucked her hair behind her ears and noted the beginnings of gray, right at her temples. She was still as beautiful as the day he first saw her.

He was angry. He was furious. Her disobedience could cost them everything. He had to make her understand that. But she was already afraid, and it was a delicate balance, this game of give and take. He needed to give her the chance to make it right.

"Why do you clean?" he asked. Her answer was instant, automatic.

"The cat. Because I have the cat. The cat sheds, so I have to clean. The fur gets everywhere, so I have to clean."

"Does the fur get everywhere?" he asked.

"Oh yes." She was watching him now, studying his face. She shook her head. "Oh no. Not everywhere. So I don't have to clean *everywhere.*"

"And where doesn't the fur get?"

"It doesn't get on the windows," she said, and he nodded. She nodded too, to herself. "It doesn't get on the windows so I don't need to clean the windows."

"That's right," he said. "You don't need to clean the windows."

He paused, waiting for her to continue. She just kept watching him, searching his face. "And where else doesn't the fur get?" he prompted.

She looked away then, at the yellow lightbulb on the ceiling, at the vacuum tracks on the carpet, at the blackout shades on the window, at the open door. She looked at the key hanging around his neck.

"The basement," she whispered.

He smiled at her benevolently. "That's right. There's no need to clean the basement. You don't want to go back down there. Can you remember that?"

She bowed her head. "Yes. I can remember that."

"That's my girl."

He still held her wrist, and he lifted her hand to his mouth and kissed the back of it. He kissed her bandaged thumb. "I'm just trying to look out for you. You work so hard and you get so tired. There's no point cleaning the places where there's no fur, now is there?"

He turned her arm over and kissed the inside of her wrist. She whispered, "No."

He trailed his lips up her arm, lingering at her elbow, at her shoulder, at her collarbone. "It's important to remember that, isn't it? We don't want to forget."

He kissed her neck, tasting the salt of her skin. She whispered breathlessly, "No."

He guided her to the bed, laid her out on the pillows. His hands found the hem of her shirt and he drew it over her head. He unclasped her bra and let it fall to the floor. He put his mouth between her breasts and cupped her flesh.

"You'll stay away from the windows?" he murmured.

She shuddered beneath his touch. "Y—yes."

"Stay away from the windows. Say it."

"I'll—I'll stay away from the windows."

"You like it inside."

"I like it inside."

"It's safe inside. You want to be safe."

She was panting, her eyelashes fluttering. Her hands were in his hair.

"Say it," he said, as he tugged down her pants. He stroked his fingers up her thighs and she gasped.

"I want—I want to be safe."

He undid his belt and cast off his pants. He stretched out on top of her. Her eyes opened, round and dark, wide and needy. He kissed her gently, then again with force.

"You're safe with me," he said as he pressed into her. She whimpered, closed her eyes, wrapped her arms around his back. He pushed deeper and she cried out. He kissed her tenderly. "You're safe with me."

HE WOKE her slowly Monday morning, after savoring a few moments watching her sleep. He stroked his fingers through her hair. He placed a kiss on the bow of her lips. She stirred, coming awake the way a flower opens to the sun. She opened to him and he smiled.

He started the shower. He invited her in. She knelt in front of him and they stayed that way until the water ran cold.

She made him breakfast, french toast with cinnamon sugar. They ate in the dining alcove. Daylight threatened at the windows but could not breach the blinds. She fixed him coffee and he kissed her for it.

He went upstairs to put on a tie. When he came down she was holding the cat and scratching behind its ears. He patted the cat. He kissed her forehead. He put the kettle on to make some tea.

"What are you going to do today?" he asked her, as a test. He knew she would give the right answer. And she did.

"Chores. Got to clean the place up."

He nodded. "Good. What else?"

She looked at him uncertainly. He didn't give her any hints. She said hesitantly, "Make dinner?"

"Of course," he said, and he smiled at her patiently. "That's what you do for me. Just like working is what I do for you, and cleaning is what you do for the cat. But what are you going to do today for yourself?"

A shy smile graced her lips, and she said softly, "Write."

"I liked your last story," he said. "You're very good at it."

Her cheeks blossomed into a soft pink and he added, "I look forward to reading the new one."

Her entire face flushed with the praise, color spreading down the pale length of her neck. He wasn't lying. She had an affinity for words. But more importantly, she found both pleasure and pride in the craft, which served him in two ways. It gave him leverage. And it kept her occupied.

It also let him know what was on her mind. Perhaps that was the greatest benefit of all.

The kettle whistled. He fixed her a cup of tea and watched as she drank it. She put the empty mug in the sink. The cat sat at her feet and meowed loudly. She picked it up and scratched behind its ears. The cat purred. She gave him a sheepish smile.

He kissed her again, lingering in it. He cupped his hand to the back of her head and held her there, until the cat squirmed between them and jumped out of her arms. They laughed, both of them, together. He drew her flush against him and held her tight.

"Have a great day," he murmured. "I'll see you tonight."

He let go of her then and walked out his front door. He locked the door behind him.

SHE WAS alone.

Except for the cat. The cat twined around her ankles and purred loudly. She picked up the cat and brought it into the kitchen with her.

The kitchen was a mess. Not from cat fur, but from her. From cooking. French toast with cinnamon sugar. She had to clean the place up. She'd made the mess, so now she had to clean. Sometimes cleaning was for her. But mostly it was for him. She knew he liked it clean.

She'd learned that long ago.

She put the cat on the floor and did the dishes. She did the dishes slowly, because there was no reason to rush. She put the dishes away and wiped the counter.

She wiped the small round dining table. She swept the floor. She looked in the fridge, then looked in the recipe book to decide what to make for dinner. She decided on alfredo. He liked alfredo. He'd told her so.

She looked for the cat but it was gone. She went into the living room. The cat was on top of the television. She put the cat on the floor and got the furniture polish and a rag from the closet. She cleaned the television and the whole inside of the cabinet so there wouldn't be any cat hair. She closed the cabinet doors so the cat wouldn't get in.

She cleaned the coffee table and the side tables with the furniture polish and rag. She polished the wooden mantle on the fireplace. She polished the wooden pony wall. She got down on her hands and knees and polished the baseboards all around the living room. She put the rag in the washer and the furniture polish away.

She got out the duster. She dusted the picture frames on the walls and the knickknacks on the mantle. She dusted the cat clock in the kitchen, the one he'd bought because he knew she liked cats. The clock was so loud. *Tik-tok, tik-tok.* The clock smiled like it knew a secret.

She went back into the living room to dust the lamps. She stopped. The lamps were watching her. She didn't want to dust the lamps, not when they were watching her. But she had to dust them, because they were watching her. She had to do her chores, had to clean the place up. She dusted the lamps as fast as she could and threw the duster back into the closet.

She took out the vacuum. She vacuumed the carpet, then swapped attachments and vacuumed the couch. She vacuumed the chairs. She used the crevice tool to vacuum along the baseboards. She put the vacuum away. She looked around.

Every day it was the same.

She filled the sink with soapy water and washed the kitchen walls. She took the clock off the wall and wiped it down before putting it back. The clock was loud in the silence of being alone.

Tik-tok. Tik-tok.

The clock's eyes went back and forth. The clock's tail went side to side. The clock's eyes went back and forth between the back door and the living room windows.

Tik-tok. Tik-tok.

The windows didn't need cleaning. They were protected by the blinds. The windows were dangerous. Stay away from the windows. There was nothing outside for her. She liked it inside.

He'd told her so.

She swept the front entry, then washed it on her hands and knees. She washed the kitchen floor. She put the cleaning supplies back in the closet where they belonged. She put fresh food down for the cat and made herself a peanut butter sandwich.

Every day it was the same.

It had always been this way.

She cleaned up the kitchen again. Washed the dishes. Wiped the counter. The cat wandered around the kitchen and she followed after it with the broom. She'd have to vacuum again, too. The cat hair just got everywhere.

She could clean again later. Right now it was time for her story. She carried the cat upstairs to the bedroom.

She opened the door and turned on the light. She put the cat on the bed and sat at her desk. She opened the middle drawer. That's where she kept the pages once she'd written them. When the story was done she would clip all the pages together and give them to him to read, but for now she kept them hidden. For now they were only for her.

She took the papers out of the middle drawer. There was a big fat stack of them. She'd only started the story last week, but she'd already written so much. The story just came pouring out. It was a story she'd heard before, or at least she thought she had, but she couldn't quite remember how it went, so she was telling it all over to herself. It was a fairy tale. The one about the princess locked in the tower.

It was a horrible story, she thought. It was very sad. The princess was stuck in the tower all day and night, and it was cold, and dark, and terribly lonely. The princess stayed very quiet, so she could listen. The princess was waiting for the prince to come. But the only one who came was the visitor.

That part was different, she thought, than the fairy tale she'd heard long ago. She thought in the fairy tale there had been a monster, maybe a dragon or some other beast, but in her story there was only a man. The man was as good as a monster, at least in the beginning. He tied the princess to the bed. He stuck the princess full of needles. He would shock her and suffocate her and say things like *this is for your own good*, and there was nothing the princess could do. She thought the visitor was going to kill her. The princess was ready to die.

That's when everything changed.

One day the visitor unlocked the tower and left it unlocked. He untied the princess from the bed and put the ropes away. There were no more needles, no more shocks. No more bag over her head. The visitor helped her up, and when she was so weak she couldn't stand, he carried the princess out of the tower and into his castle. He gave her food and a bath and brought her to his bed. He laid with her, and there was pleasure like she'd never known. He was kind to her. He looked after her. And when she was stronger, he began to teach her. How to cook. How to clean. How dangerous it was beyond the castle. The princess realized he had rescued her. He had been her prince all along.

It was a happy ending, she thought, and a happy ending counted for a lot. But it wasn't the whole story. And now that she'd written the ending, she thought it was time to write the beginning.

To write about the princess before she was in the tower.

Before she met the visitor.

Before.

Because it hadn't always been this way.

She put the pages of her story on the desk beside her typewriter. She rubbed her temples. She'd been getting headaches lately, whenever she wrote. She'd been getting them since she started the story. But she wanted to keep writing, wanted to finish it. She wanted to find out what happened to the princess.

She skimmed the pages she wrote last time. A dull ache settled at the base of her skull. She put a new sheet of paper in the typewriter and cranked it through. Spikes of pain shot between her ears. She put her fingers on the keys and she thought, thought hard, about where the princess was before she was in the tower. She started to type. Her head squeezed. Her eyes crossed. She cried out in pain as the room shone and spun. She fell from her chair to the floor. The last thing she saw, before it all went pitch black, was the cat jumping off the bed. It moved toward her, tail flicking back and forth like a hungry flame. It purred loudly, like the rumbling of an engine.

HE CAME home after work with a gift for her.

It was logical, after all. Part of the give and take. She had done well, so she would be rewarded. And rewards would encourage like behavior.

The gift was for her. She earned it. She deserved it. But if he was honest with himself, it was also for him. To make himself feel better after resorting to punishment. He did not like to see her punished. He did not want to do it again.

But he would if it was necessary. He had come too far to turn soft.

He unlocked the door, the new DVD tucked under his arm. The latest Disney movie. She enjoyed them very much. She would be in the kitchen, cooking supper, and he would join her there, holding the movie behind his back, and he would kiss her and surprise her with it, and her eyes would go wide because new movies were a special treat, and they would eat supper together and then afterward curl up on the couch in front of the TV, and all would be well.

He didn't have to get any further than the front entry to know all was not well.

The kitchen was dark. The living room was dark. There were no sounds of cooking. No smell of supper.

She wasn't there.

Panic took him swiftly to the back door, to check the lock. Still secured. He turned on every light and searched the main floor, just to be sure. No sign of her. He rushed up the stairs to the bedroom, cursing himself. He should have checked on her today. He should have checked. Work had been busy, but still he should have checked. It would only have taken a minute. Instead he'd held onto a vain hope that the crisis was passed.

Goddammit, he should have *checked*.

The bedroom door was ajar, yellow light at the seams. He flung the door open and burst into the room.

She was in bed, curled up on her side. She faced away from him. The cat lay at her feet.

She was tired, that was all. She'd just been tired. He went around the bed and gently shook her.

"Honey?"

She was pale, paler than usual, pale in a way that spoke of more than fatigue. She hadn't stirred. He shook her again.

"Honey."

His gaze fell to the bedsheets, drawn up to her chin. A single spot marred the pure white bedding, a perfect circle of crimson red. His heart filled his throat and he ripped the bedding back, prepared for anything. But there was nothing. She was fine. Her sleeping form was wholly pristine.

When he looked at her face she was looking back at him.

"I—" He had to swallow, had to give himself a moment. He wasn't one to lose his composure.

"I thought you might have been sick," he said. "You look feverish. Are you ill?"

"Just tired," she whispered, and her voice rasped like she'd been screaming. His eyes were drawn to the circle of red.

"Let me look at you."

He helped her sit up, helped her pull her nightgown over her head. The nightgown was a clean white. Beneath the nightgown her skin was white too. He ran his hands over her, turned her, lifted her arms up and down. No cuts. No marks. He took hold of her chin.

"Open your mouth."

She complied. Pearly teeth grinned back at him, as white as her skin, the nightgown, the bedding. But on her tongue he could see marks like she'd bitten down. The corners of her mouth showed paper-thin cuts. He gave her back her nightgown.

"Just relax. I'll bring you some tea."

He left her in bed and went quietly down the stairs. He stepped on something hard. The DVD case. He must have dropped it on his way up. He opened the case and snapped the DVD in half. He threw it in the trash.

HE LAID awake that night into the witching hours. When he was certain she was asleep he got out of bed. He went to her writing desk. He opened the middle drawer. He took the pages into the bathroom and turned on the light.

He would not do this. Normally he would not do this. There was so much of her life he had control of, and to grant her this one privacy seemed like a small concession. Especially when he knew she would share it with him eventually. Because she wanted to. There was mutual benefit in that.

But tonight he needed to know, because he hadn't checked on her during the day. He'd been foolish. He'd made a mistake. This was not the time for reward, or false hope. The crisis had not passed.

Perhaps, all these years later, it had never passed at all.

He began to read the pages.

His stomach sank.

This was not her usual story. Her usual stories were fluff and happy endings. Children's stories, like the movies they watched. Nothing bad happened in her stories.

But *this* story...good God.

He set the pages on the sink as he finished them, face-down. He couldn't bear to look at them again. He'd tried to forget. He'd hoped she had too. But nothing was ever truly forgotten, was it? Nothing ever went away.

He came to the end of the story, but still another page remained. The page felt rough, like it had been crinkled. Hard, like it had been wet and then dried. He knew what he would see as he set aside the last page of the story. It was all he could do not to look away.

Against the white of the page were bright splotches of blood. There were bite marks on the edges. Across the top of the page was a paragraph of pure gibberish, and below that, in all caps, repeated line after line, was a message:

I REMEMBER

I REMEMBER

I REMEMBER

He turned the light off in the bathroom and returned the pages to their drawer. He got back into bed and laid next to her. He did not sleep.

IN THE morning he had to go to work. He had to. His was not the sort of job you could miss. Not even when your wife was ill. Especially not when your wife was ill.

Especially when everyone knew you didn't have a wife.

He looked tired, he knew. The sort of tired that invited questions. And he did not like the thought of leaving her alone all day. But his was not the sort of job you could miss.

He got out of bed carefully, as not to disturb her. He showered and dressed quietly, as not to disturb her. He went down to the kitchen and put on the kettle. He made tea. A whole pot of it. He brought the pot and a mug upstairs.

The bedroom door was closed. He opened it. The light was off. He turned it on. She was still in bed, curled up on her side, nothing visible but her dark mass of hair.

He set the mug on the nightstand next to the bed. He filled the mug with tea and watched steam curl and disappear. He set the teapot on her writing desk. He sat beside her on the bed and watched her.

Assessed her.

Considered his options.

He still found her attractive, there was no question about that. He had been drawn to her from the start, and time had only strengthened his attachment to her. He was invested in her. He was happy with her. Having her was worth the risk.

She had always been worth the risk.

But that didn't mean he wouldn't act. He would take measures to keep her safe. To keep them both safe. To keep them together.

Give and take. Punishment and reward. Actions and consequences.

For better or for worse.

He laid his hand on her forehead and smoothed her hair back. She opened her eyes slowly, groggily. He smiled kindly.

"I'm going to work now," he told her. "I made you tea."

He motioned for her to sit up and he gave her the steaming mug. He watched while she drank it, not moving until she'd drank it all. When she'd finished he refilled it from the teapot on her writing desk.

"Have some more," he told her. "Drink it all up."

She finished the mug. He filled it again. She finished the third mug. Her eyes drowsed shut.

He tucked her snugly beneath the blankets and kissed the crown of her head. She couldn't hear him anymore but he spoke anyway.

"I'm sorry for what happened yesterday. It was my fault. I should have checked on you. I'll check on you today, as often as I can. I'll be home right after work. I'll take care of you. I promise."

He left the light on in the bedroom, glancing up at the bare bulb as he passed beneath it. He left the door open so the cat could come in. He left for work. He locked the deadbolt soundly behind him.

HIS OFFICE was stark. Sparse. Small, but it came with a private bathroom and a reception area. He didn't have a receptionist. He thought it best to handle things himself.

His schedule lay on the blotter, packed from 8 to 5. He'd have scarcely a moment to catch his breath, much less check up on her. He'd find time. He'd make time. He wouldn't let yesterday happen again, even though, if all went well, she'd spend the entire day asleep. He'd made the tea strong this morning, used up the last of what he had. Better refill now before his patients started coming in.

He took a silver key from his wallet and unlocked the corner cabinet. This was where he kept the samples. The samples were why he did what he did, working long hours, seeing so many patients, being generous with his prescriptions. The more patients he brought in the more popular he was with the big pharma reps, and the more popular he was the more samples he got. Free medication, no prescription required.

He did it for her. All of it.

He opened the cabinet's top drawer. Here were the benzodiazepines. They kept her relaxed. Sedated. They also caused modest amnesia. He'd been using them for years, and with great success. Or so he thought. The message at the end of her story suggested otherwise.

No matter. He'd simply give her more.

He found what he needed and put the boxes in his briefcase. He opened the second drawer. Here were the heavy hitters. The antipsychotics. Asenapine, quetiapine, clozapine. Lurasidone. Risperidone. Lithium. He'd used them heavily in the beginning, then gradually weaned her off as he transitioned to operant conditioning. She was on a low dose now, just enough to keep her stable. Or so he thought. The blood at the end of her story suggested otherwise.

He could fix that. He'd simply give her more.

In the bottom drawer were the antidepressants. Prolonged use of the benzos could bring her too low, and he did not want that. Would not allow that. Would fight that as hard as he could. He was treating her, after all. He was looking after her. He threw a few boxes of fluoxetine into his briefcase, then added a couple boxes of zolpidem. Just in case treatment took longer than he thought.

Just in case he needed her to sleep.

He locked the cabinet and placed the key back his wallet. He closed his briefcase and snapped the latches. He slid the briefcase beneath his desk. He opened the door to his office and waited for his first arrival.

SHE SLEPT. She lay still. She did not move, she could not move. Her limbs felt heavy. Her mind felt thick. She drifted. She dreamed.

She had a terrible nightmare.

41

But when she woke up it was gone. All that remained was the ghost of a memory. All there was was the cat curled at her feet. It lifted its head, its eyes reflecting the lightbulb's glow like fire on water. It purred, like the rumbling of an engine.

She closed her eyes. Her head was beginning to hurt.

HE STOPPED at the store on the way home to pick up soup. He chose cream of broccoli. He went home and parked in the driveway and brought the soup and his briefcase into the house. He left them in the kitchen while he went upstairs to see her.

She was in bed, curled up on her side. Just the same way she'd been each time he checked on her. The cat was there, wrapped around her feet. He shooed it away and woke her.

"Come downstairs. I brought you soup."

She was slow to get up, clumsy when she moved. The high dosage this morning had turned her to jelly. He helped her down the stairs, one arm secure around her waist. He sat her at the table while he warmed the soup on the stovetop. When it was ready he fed it to her, one spoonful at a time.

He let her rest on the couch in the living room while he tidied up. When he'd finished he put on a movie. He sat beside her and she sagged against him, her head resting on his shoulder. He put his arm around her. He held her close. When the movie was over he carried her to bed.

HE WOKE from a dead sleep in the middle of the night to a

noise in the kitchen.

The room was dark. He couldn't see anything. He could only feel.

She wasn't there.

He got out of bed. The bedroom door was closed. He opened it. The hallway was dark, but not as dark as the bedroom. He could see the top of the stairs. He stood at the top of the stairs and listened.

Chop-chop-chop.

He descended the stairs. No lights were on, but light came in from the street through the window above the door. Light gathered at the edges of the drawn blinds. Light crept in through the cracks between the blinds and made silver slits on the wall. Light drew shadows from the furniture and reflections from the glass. Light glinted in the kitchen and he heard *chop-chop-chop*.

He entered the kitchen.

She stood at the counter, a white spectre in a monochromatic room. Her nightgown swayed around her ankles. Her dark hair was tied back. In her hand she held a meat cleaver. It was half the length of her arm.

Chop-chop-chop.

She had something on the cutting board. In the dark he couldn't see what it was. She lifted the cleaver a few inches off the board and brought it down again. Again.

Chop-chop-chop.

"Honey?"

She didn't turn to him, didn't seem to hear him at all. Up went the cleaver, then back down. *Chop-chop-chop.*

"Honey."

The cleaver was half the length of her arm. The blade was as big as his hand. She didn't hear him, she didn't notice him at all. He turned on the light.

She was sleepwalking.

Her eyes were open but vacant, dazed and glassy. She didn't react to the light. She lifted the cleaver and brought it back down. *Chop-chop-chop.*

She was cutting a lamp cord.

The lamp was on the counter, lying on its side. It had come from the living room. Bits of cord scattered the ground at her feet. She ran out of cord on the cutting board, dragged the lamp closer, and kept going.

Chop-chop-chop.

He couldn't take his eyes off that cleaver.

Chop-chop-chop. She slid the cord forward. *Chop-chop-chop.* The blade missed her fingers by a hair.

Sweat moistened his forehead. His heart ached with the suspense. He moved forward, hands outstretched, waiting for the right moment to catch her wrists, to stop her before—

She turned on him with the cleaver raised. He froze. Her eyes were glassy. Her face was blanched. Her lips moved soundlessly, over and over. Then they spread into a smile. She whispered, almost sing-song:

"I re-*memmm*-ber."

Her eyes rolled up in her head. She dropped the cleaver and crumpled to the floor.

HE SAT in the hallway outside the bedroom, his back to the door. He did not drink. He did not smoke. He wished desperately now that he did. He wished for something to steady his trembling hands, to still his racing heart, to take his mind off the problem, if only for a moment. But he had only one vice. And it was her.

He pressed his hands to his face and breathed deep.

The lamps. Lamps plural, because there had been two. She'd chopped up another one before he'd gotten down there. They were both from the living room. They were both table lamps. She hadn't gotten to the floor lamp yet, which was lucky, because that's where it was.

His surveillance camera.

One of three that let him check on her during the day.

She couldn't have known. She *couldn't* have known. The camera was tiny, barely visible even if you knew where to look. She'd never seen it, never seen any of them.

Yet she thought the lamps were watching her.

And she'd been right.

He tried to see the positive. She'd killed two lamps, but all his cameras had survived. It was possible she didn't know about the other two. The one in the kitchen. The one in the bedroom. She'd only said *lamps*. Perhaps the others were safe.

They would have to be. He wasn't about to turn them off. Now now. Not after…

Good God.

The meat cleaver.

He could still see it flashing up and down on the cutting board. Could see her raising it against him. Could see it fall to the floor, and her fall on top of it. He'd let out a cry so terrible it made his eyes water, and he'd fallen to his knees, pleading with her not to die. He'd waited for blood. There was none. He'd searched her for cuts. There were none. The cleaver had fallen on its side. The blade had not left a single mark.

He'd cried then, with relief. It was the first time he'd cried in years.

Since the beginning.

Since he'd rescued her from that hospital.

She was asleep now, well and truly asleep. He'd roused her long enough to give her a cup of tea. She wouldn't remember anything in the morning, or so he hoped. Sleepwalkers rarely did. The medicine would help with that too. And perhaps it was out of her system now, the fear that had driven her subconscious to action. Perhaps the worst was over.

He'd thought that before.

Better to be safe.

He got up from the hallway floor and went down to the kitchen. He gathered all the lamp bits and threw them in the trash. He took the trash and dumped it in the bin. He brought the bin to the curb. He went back inside the house.

He went silently up the stairs and opened the door to the bedroom. He paused, watching, waiting. She did not stir. He went into the closet and found his shoe at the back. He lifted the insole and removed the key. He returned silently to the kitchen.

He took the meat cleaver and put it in a box. He took the knife block and put it in the box. He opened all the drawers and the cupboards and found everything sharp and put it in the box. He unlocked the door to the basement. He put the box at the foot of the stairs. He locked the door again and checked it to be sure. He turned off the lights in the kitchen and went up to the bedroom. He put the key back in the shoe and tucked the shoe away deep in the closet. He closed the closet door and got into bed.

It was the second night he did not sleep.

HE WAS up early the next morning, long before he'd usually wake her. He was down in the kitchen, sorting through his briefcase. He hadn't unpacked it the night before. He unpacked it now. He studied what he had and weighed his options. Considered her symptoms. He settled on a strong cocktail and crushed the pills into powder. He put the kettle on to make tea.

He heard footsteps upstairs.

He ran, but quietly. Fast, but without making a sound. The bedroom door was closed, but it opened silently on its hinges. She was out of bed. The bathroom door was shut. No more sounds came. She was quiet.

Good God, he'd forgotten about the razors.

He took hold of the doorknob. It was locked. He reared back and kicked the door in. The hollow wood splintered spectacularly.

She was at the sink, hair piled atop her head, her pink toothbrush hanging limply from her mouth. Toothpaste dribbled down her chin. Her face was white.

"I—"

His throat caught. He couldn't speak, couldn't produce another sound. He stepped into the bathroom and she shrank back against the wall. They stared at each other. Toothpaste dribbled down her chin.

"I didn't mean to," he said. It was barely a whisper.

Downstairs the kettle whistled. He left the bathroom and shut the broken door behind him. He went down to the kitchen and made the tea.

"Do your chores today." That's what he told her. "Clean everything up. But don't make dinner. I'll bring something home. Do you understand?"

She nodded. He said, "No writing, either. Read a book, or watch a movie if you like. Do you hear me?"

She nodded. He handed her a mug. "Drink your tea."

She did. He kissed her, hard, his hand firm on the back of her head. He kissed her hard and for too long. He held her tight and for too long. Then he left, and he locked the door behind him.

She went straight into the bathroom and threw up.

She brushed her teeth. She spat into the sink. She could still taste it, beneath the toothpaste, beneath the vomit. Something bitter. Something metallic. Her tea was wrong. He'd given her the wrong tea.

He'd broken the door.

49

He was scaring her.

Something was wrong.

It was her fault.

She'd done something wrong, but she didn't know what. She didn't know when. She didn't know why. She never knew why. She only knew she should do what he wanted.

She started on her chores.

She did the dishes. She put them away. She wiped the counter. She wiped the table. She swept the floor. She opened the cleaning closet and got out the duster. She went to the living room. She stopped.

The lamps were gone.

Two lamps were gone.

He'd gotten rid of the lamps for her.

She was so grateful she wanted to cry.

She dusted with a smile on her face. She smiled as she dusted the last lamp. It was next, she thought. He'd take care of it next. She dusted really well, so he would be pleased. She dusted the baseboards and the furniture feet and inside the little knickknacks on the fireplace mantle. She put the duster away and got a rag and the furniture polish. She polished the coffee table and the two side tables and the baseboards and the furniture feet. She polished the small round dining table. She polished the two dining chairs. She put the polish away and filled the kitchen sink with soapy water. She washed the kitchen floor and the front entry. She washed the knickknacks from the fireplace. She washed the walls. She took the clock off the wall and wiped it down and put it back. The clock's eyes went back and forth. The clock's tail went side to side. The clock smiled like it knew a secret.

Tik-tok. Tik-tok.

She drained the sink and scrubbed it out and then made herself a peanut butter sandwich. She fed a corner of it to the cat. She looked at the clock.

There was still a lot of time left before he came back.

She wanted to write. It was her writing time. She hadn't written for two days. But he'd told her not to. He'd specifically told her not to. She didn't know why, but that's what he'd said. He said read a book. He said watch a movie. He said no writing.

He'd gotten rid of the lamps for her.

He'd kicked in the door.

He'd given her the wrong tea.

But he got rid of the lamps. She should do what he wanted. It was better to do what he wanted.

She did the dishes. She put them away. She wiped the table. She wiped the counter. She went into the living room and sat on the couch. The blinds were drawn and the daylight was too weak to penetrate. She left the remaining lamp on so she would have enough light. She took a book from the drawer of the coffee table and began to read. The cat hopped up next to her and curled against her leg. Its ears flicked back and forth, like twin candles in the wind. It purred loudly, like the rumbling of an engine.

She put a hand to her forehead. Her headache was coming back.

HE WAS at work. His schedule was packed. But in the breath between appointments he closed his office door. He ducked into the private bathroom. He took out his cell phone and opened the app.

The first camera was a sea of black. That was the bedroom camera. That meant the light was off. Either she was in bed or she wasn't in the room. He swiped to the next camera.

This was the kitchen camera. This one was on. The overhead light in the kitchen was on, but the camera that fed off it showed an empty room. He swiped to the last camera.

This was the living room camera, hidden on the last lamp. The lamp was on, which meant the camera was on. And there she was. She was on the couch, a book in her lap, the cat tucked against her side. The book was closed. Her head lolled against the cushions.

She was asleep.

He heard the bell jingle in his reception area. His next patient had arrived. He closed the app and put his phone away and returned to his office. He opened the door. He called the patient in. He thought of her sleeping on the couch, and he smiled.

Everything was going to be fine.

SHE WAS dreaming. It was a dream. It wasn't real. It wasn't like this anymore.

It was a memory.

She was in a room, a white room. Sitting on a white bed. The white floors were cold so she wore a pair of white slippers. A white gown that tied up in the back. She was sitting on the bed. She was waiting.

"Knock knock, you have a visitor."

The door opened and he came in. He wore white too, a long white coat. He had white gloves. He had a clipboard. He had a smile.

She didn't smile back.

He told her to stand. She stood. He turned her around. She complied. He took off her white gown and ran his hands over every inch of her. She didn't move. He nodded in approval and gave her back the gown. She let it fall to the floor. She looked at him. He looked away. He looked back. He looked all over her. He picked up the gown and dressed her in it. He made some notes on his clipboard and gestured for her to sit.

"No wounds," he said. "That's good. That's progress."

She didn't answer.

"What will I see when I check your mouth?"

She didn't respond.

"Lie down, please."

She stretched out on the narrow white bed. She hung her hands off the sides and spread her legs. He strapped her down at the wrists and ankles.

"Now then," he said. "Don't bite."

She looked up at the ceiling. He slid his hands beneath her head. She felt him unlock the straps, and then it came off.

The muzzle.

He set it aside.

"Open wide," he said, and she licked her lips. Ran her tongue along her teeth. She opened her mouth and let his fingers in.

53

He ran his fingers along her gums. She felt the warmth of his hands. He checked her tongue and the roof of her mouth. She tasted the latex of his gloves. He swept his thumbs up the insides of her cheeks. Saliva pooled at the back of her throat.

He withdrew his hands. She swallowed, and licked her lips.

"That's excellent," he said. "Nearly a month without an incident." He made some notes on his clipboard. "Now then. Time for your medicine."

He reached into his pocket and took out a small bottle. He uncapped it. He shook out two pills.

"It's not working," she told him. "Your treatment. Nothing's changed."

He frowned. "Of course it has. You've stopped."

"Because you stopped me. You can't stop me forever."

His frown deepened. His eyes hardened. He leaned over her, so close she could see the veins in his throat. So close she could hear his heart beating.

"I can stop you," he said. "I can save you. You're sick. You don't know what you're doing. But I'm going to save you."

"I know what I'm doing," she said. "I know what I need. And it's not this."

"Take your medicine."

She opened her mouth. He put the pills on her tongue one by one. One was bitter, the other metallic. She chewed them. She swallowed. He checked her mouth to be sure.

"He wanted to, you know," she said. "He asked me to. It was his choice."

She looked up at him, tensing, drawing the restraints tight at her wrists. He looked down at her. He put his hand on her forehead and smoothed back her hair. He brushed his hand down her cheek.

"No one chooses that," he said. "Just like you didn't choose this. It's not your fault. You're going to get better. Just let me help you."

"He said that too," she told him, whispering it. "He just wanted to help." She licked her lips and looked up at him, and she whispered, "I want you next."

He held his hand against her cheek. He stroked his thumb along her brow. He bent down and kissed her, and his taste was as sweet as sugar. She nipped lightly at his lip. He pulled back. He checked his lip for blood. There was none.

Of course not.

Not yet.

He picked up the muzzle and fit it to her face, slipping the guard between her teeth. He fastened the straps. He locked them shut. He freed her wrists and ankles and she sat up.

"I'll be back to bring you lunch," he said, and he smiled again. His hand went unconsciously to his lip. "The treatment's helping you. You'll see. Someday you'll understand."

She didn't answer. She had a muzzle on her mouth.

He gave her one last lingering look and then he left. The door locked automatically behind him.

WORK WAS busy. His schedule was packed. He liked it that way, he liked to keep himself occupied. It had been his routine for years. In the beginning it was different. He hadn't worked at all. The hospital was gone so there was no place to work. He wouldn't have had time anyway. She'd needed him. She'd needed everything he had to give. She had been difficult, in the beginning. But she got better. And when she was better he went back to work, for himself, because the hospital was still gone. But there was still a demand for his services. There were so many of them, so many people who needed his help. All those poor, broken people. All those lost, desperate souls.

What was it Lou called them?

Crazies.

They were his crazies.

He could help them, the way he'd helped her. He could save them, the way he'd saved her. He could work longer now, could help more of them, because of her. Because he trusted her. He could spend the day at work and know all would be well when he got home.

All had been well for years.

All had been well until last week.

He was lying to himself if he thought all remained well.

But he would fix it. He would. He would clear his schedule for next week. He would stay home every day with her. He would stop this. He would bring her back. He would save her. Again.

He would spend his last breath saving her.

His last appointment had just finished. His next appointment was about to begin. He slipped into the bathroom and took out his phone. He checked the app. There she was, on the couch, still asleep. He allowed himself a smile.

All was still well.

For now.

He closed the app. He put his phone away. He settled behind his desk. The next appointment was about to begin.

SHE OPENED her eyes.

She saw flames. She saw fire.

She heard screaming.

They were in the halls. They were running in the halls. She got off her narrow bed and looked through the small window on her door and saw patients running in the halls. She saw the fire. She saw them fall. She heard the screaming.

She tried her door. It was locked. It was always locked. She wasn't free to roam the ward like other patients were. She stayed here and the doctors came to her. She saw the doctors out there, and the nurses, and they were running too. They were all running away.

She was going to die here. She knew immediately she was going to die.

She went back to her bed and laid down.

She heard sirens outside the hospital. She saw smoke creep beneath her door. The hallway was orange. The air was thick. She heard the screaming.

She closed her eyes.

Her door opened.

"Be quiet," he said, as he entered the room. "Don't

57

move," he said, as he swaddled her in a wet blanket. "Be quiet. Don't move. I'll get you out of here."

He picked her up and ran into the hall.

The air was hot. The air was thick. She couldn't see, she had the blanket over her head. She couldn't speak, she had the muzzle over her mouth. She stayed still. She heard his feet pounding as he ran. She heard him gasping as he ran. She heard his heart race.

She heard the screams.

Then they were gone.

The air was cold. The air was thin. She shivered beneath the wet blanket. She heard his footsteps slow to a walk. She heard him grunt as he adjusted his grip. She heard a click and a pop, and then she was set down. She was set down on her side. She heard him above her.

"Be quiet. Don't move. I'm getting you out of here."

She heard a door shut above her, then she heard nothing. She heard nothing. She shivered. She waited.

Then she heard it.

The rumbling of an engine.

SHE HEARD it. She heard the engine rumbling.

She felt the engine rumbling. She couldn't stand it anymore.

She screamed.

She screamed, and she twisted frantically in the wet blanket. She screamed, and she lashed out blindly. She fell, still screaming. She hurt her arm. She screamed some more. She shivered and sobbed and she rocked back and forth, and eventually she opened her eyes.

The rumbling had stopped.

She was cold, but there was no wet blanket. She was alone, but she wasn't in the trunk. She was at home. She was in the living room. She had fallen off the couch.

She'd been dreaming, nothing more. A terrible dream. A horrible nightmare.

She was home. She was safe.

It was only a dream.

Her arm hurt. She looked down.

Three long marks in perfect parallel went from her elbow to her wrist. In her hand she clutched bits of fur.

The cat. She'd hurt the cat. She looked for the cat and there it was, on the other side of the room. Its hackles were up. It spat at her. She called to it but it fled the room. It disappeared up the stairs.

She'd hurt the cat. She hadn't meant to. But she'd been dreaming, she'd had a terrible dream, and the cat had rumbled—

Like an engine.

Sharp pain split through her skull and she whimpered. She held her head in both hands and curled into a ball. It was a dream, it was only a dream. It was only a dream. It was only a dream. She said the words but not out loud. She only said them in her head. Her teeth chattered. Her arm hurt.

Her arm was really starting to hurt.

She looked down at the long marks on her arm. They were red. They were swollen. They were oozing drops of blood.

She knew what he'd do, if he were here. He'd clean the scratches. He'd bandage them up. He'd make her change, make her put on something with long sleeves, just to be careful, he'd say. Then he'd make her a cup of tea and she'd fall asleep.

But he wasn't here.

She looked down at her arm, at the marks, at the drops of blood. They looked like jewels, like rubies glittering on her skin. They were beautiful. Lovely. Perfect.

She put her mouth over the scratches and sucked.

She closed her eyes. She savored.

It was the sweetest thing she'd ever tasted.

She sucked until no more blood would come out. Then she dug into the scratches with her fingertips and forced the skin further apart. Blood blossomed, ran in rivers down her arm. She lapped it up. If her arm still hurt she couldn't feel it. She felt only pleasure. She knew only bliss.

After a great length of time she stopped. She was satisfied. She was happy. And her headache was gone.

She hadn't felt this good since…since…

Before.

Since they found her with her lover. Since they sent her to that place. Since he got his hands on her and changed her, made her forget. She hadn't felt this good in years. And now she knew why.

She smiled.

I remember.

She stood. She was a little dizzy, a little unsteady on her feet. She climbed the stairs. She went into the bathroom. She needed to take care of her arm. It was a gruesome, bloody mess. She didn't mind. It had been worth it.

But she'd better not let him see.

She washed her arm with soap and water. She patted it dry. She took a tube of ointment from the medicine cabinet and smeared it all over the wounds. She wrapped her arm tightly with gauze. She changed her shirt, dressing herself in long sleeves. She put a sweater over top to hide the bulk. She checked herself for blood and started back downstairs.

She heard meowing behind her and stopped.

The cat.

It sat near the laundry closet, tail swishing back and forth. It meowed pitifully. She crouched.

"Here, kitty, kitty."

The cat stood but didn't approach. Its tail swished back and forth. She crooned to it, beckoning with her fingers.

"Come on, kitty. Come here."

The cat hesitated. She could see a patch of skin through its fur, right on the back of its neck. Poor thing. She hadn't meant to. She gave up calling to it and sat down on the carpet. She waited.

The cat crept toward her. She didn't move. The cat drew nearer. She stayed perfectly still. The cat came right up to her and weaved around her, rubbing against her side. It nudged her with its head and she scratched gently behind its ears.

The cat climbed into her lap and settled there. Its tail swished back and forth, like a dancing flame. It purred, like the rumbling of an engine.

She moved her hand to the base of its neck.

The cat meowed, and she shushed it kindly. She stroked

the bare patch of skin and felt its warmth. She put her hand to the cat's chest and felt its heart beat. She liked the cat. It had been her companion for years. But she'd been mistaken earlier. She wasn't satisfied. Not with her own blood. Not after a famine of so long. She needed her strength.

Because she'd only just begun.

"Good kitty." She held tightly to the cat's torso. "Good kitty." She took hold of the cat's delicate neck. The cat purred like the rumbling of an engine. She licked her lips.

"Good kitty."

The rumbling stopped.

HE CAME through the front door and there she was, curled up on the couch with a book. She looked up. She smiled. It was a moment before he smiled in return.

Her dark hair was down, brushed to perfect glossiness. Her complexion had color. Her eyes were bright. She looked well, better than she had in some time. She was awake. Aware. Alert.

Not at all what he'd expected after changing her medication.

He shut the door. He locked it. He crossed the living room to where she was curled up on the couch. He bent over to kiss her. She kissed him back. He was surprised she kissed him back. She had been terrified of him this morning.

That nap must have done her a world of good.

"How are you?" he asked. It was as close as he could get to *I'm sorry*.

She looked up at him. She smiled. "I'm fine."

"You feel all right?" He touched her cheek. It was as close as he could get to *please forgive me*.

She smiled at him. Her cheek was rosy beneath his touch. He stroked its smoothness. He cherished its warmth.

"I feel wonderful," she said softly. "You have no idea."

She closed her book and stood up and she kissed him. She kissed him deeply. She caressed his chest. He felt himself respond to her and he set down the bag of takeout he carried. The bag was hot and the food smelled wonderful. He kicked it aside and put his hands on her.

She unbuttoned his shirt. He shrugged it off and pulled her to his chest. She unbuttoned his pants. He kicked them off and sank onto the couch. She slid between his knees. He buried his hands in her hair. She took him in. Her mouth was hot but it made him shiver. Her lips were soft but they made him ache. She pulled away.

"Don't," he said. Panted. "Don't stop," he said. Begged.

She stood. He watched her hungrily. She took her pants off. He couldn't look away. She climbed into his lap and he took hold of her hips, and he thrust into her forcefully as he lost all control. Her mouth found his and she gasped into it, moaned into it. She clung to him and he gripped her that much tighter. He ravaged her. Worshipped her. He emptied himself in her and then fell backward, spent. She was still kissing him, so hard his mouth hurt. He kissed her back.

He tasted blood.

He stood so quickly she tumbled to the floor.

He touched his lip. It was painful, swollen. His fingers came back red. He looked at her, half-naked on the carpet. She looked up at him and licked her lips.

He whispered, "What did you do?"

She only smiled. His blood made her teeth gleam red.

He seized her by the arm and forced her up the stairs. He brought her into the bathroom and stood her under the stark white light. He checked her legs quickly, already knowing the wound wasn't there. She would have hidden it.

She wasn't wearing that sweater this morning.

He drew the sweater up and over her head, and then he saw the bulk on her forearm. She had another shirt covering it. He removed that too. She stood quietly as he worked. He heard the wet smack of her lips. His bare skin prickled from head to toe.

Slowly and with great care, he unwrapped the bandage on her arm. When he saw it he gasped. Her arm was mutilated, the skin split, craters gouged deep. It was red, inflamed, no doubt painful beyond belief, yet she gave no indication of discomfort. She simply stood there. Waiting. Smiling.

It was then he noticed the marks beneath the mess. The three long scratches in perfect parallel. He felt himself go white.

"Honey," he whispered, "where's the cat?"

She grinned. Her teeth gleamed red.

His hands trembled. His heart skittered. He said weakly, "Let me make you some tea."

SHE WAS in bed. Asleep. She'd accepted the tea. She'd drank two cups and then she'd gone upstairs. He'd needed a moment before he could follow. He was still reeling from what she said, perfectly clear, looking him right in the eye.

I remember.

He had failed.

She'd gone upstairs alone, and he'd stayed in the kitchen, leaning on the counter for support. Ten years of his life invested in her. Ten years of effort, of sacrifice, of secrets. Ten years of lies and keeping up appearances. Ten years of thinking he'd saved her, and now the crushing realization that he had failed. But that wasn't even the worst part. The thing that was worst, the thing that threatened to buckle his knees out from under him, was the knowledge he'd have to do it again. From the beginning. Start over. Rebuild from the ground up. He'd been too easy on her, he could see that now. He hadn't broken her thoroughly enough. So he'd have to start again. He had to break her down so she could be rebuilt. So she could be saved.

So, in the end, they could be together.

There was no other way.

He would start again, and he would get it right this time. He would be relentless. Ruthless. For however long it took. Ten years was nothing.

Not when you were in love.

She'd gone upstairs alone, and he'd stayed in the kitchen, leaning on the counter for support while he hardened his resolve. Then he'd followed. He had found her in the bathroom, brushing her teeth. When she finished he bandaged her arm. He put her to bed. He sat beside her and stroked her hair until she fell asleep. He sat there another hour to be sure.

Now he got up. He went to the closet. He went deep into

the closet and found his shoe at the back. He lifted the insole. He withdrew the key. He went down to the basement and began his preparations.

SHE WAS not asleep. She only pretended to be. She'd drank two cups of tea, but she'd gone straight into the bathroom and threw them up while he remained in the kitchen. When he came up she'd been brushing her teeth. He put her to bed, and he sat with her a long time while she feigned sleep, but eventually he'd gotten up. He'd gone around the bed. He'd gone into the closet. Then he'd gone downstairs.

Now she was waiting. She was waiting for him to return. After a great length of time he finally did. He went into the closet. He got into bed. She listened to him fall asleep, and she smiled to herself in the darkness.

H E WOKE her in the morning, tenderly, as he always did. He smoothed back her hair. He traced the curve of her cheek. He kissed her. He kissed her softly because his lip was still swollen. He kissed her until she kissed him back.

He started the shower. He invited her in. The water was warm. The bathroom filled with steam. He watched the water course over her body. He used his fingers to bring her to her knees. He knelt behind her and entered her, holding her as he moved. It was the last time he could be with her for weeks, maybe months. He would not let this phase of their life together end on last night.

He made her breakfast, french toast with cinnamon sugar. They ate in the dining alcove. Outside the day was fiercely bright, but inside it was simply a soft glow. The blinds cast golden stripes on the wall. The clock *tik-tok*ed to fill the silence.

He did the dishes after breakfast and put on the kettle. He made her tea and watched her drink it. He made her drink the whole pot. He watched her eyelids droop with every cup. When she'd finished he carried her to the couch.

"I'll be back in an hour," he told her, stroking her hair. "Read a book while I'm gone. If you're tired it's okay to sleep."

She nodded. Otherwise she did not move.

Outside the day was fiercely bright, and the living room was filled with a soft glow. He turned the lamp on anyway. He went back to her and took her in his arms.

"I love you," he murmured. "Do you know that? I love you. Do you understand?"

She nodded. She laid her head on his shoulder. He held her tight and then let her go.

His briefcase waited near the entry. He picked it up and walked out the door. He locked the door carefully behind him.

SHE WAITED until he'd locked the door, then stuck her finger down her throat and retched. Her head was foggy. Her limbs were lead. She'd had too much tea, she couldn't wait. She needed it now.

She peeled the bandage off her arm. Her hands were clumsy. Her movements were slow. Her arm was slick with ointment. She rubbed it off. She brought her arm to her mouth and bit down.

Pain came first, and it sliced through the fog. Then came

pleasure as her blood began to flow. She drank it in greedily and the fog went away. She found her strength and sat up.

An hour, he'd said. That wasn't much time. She took care of her arm first, redressing and rewrapping it. Then she cleaned up the vomit near the couch.

At last, at long last, she went into the bedroom. She opened the closet door. She searched the closet from front to back, and at the back she found a shoe. Inside the shoe was a key on a leather cord.

She smiled, and her smile gleamed red.

HIS FIRST session had come and gone by the time he reached the clinic. His next patient was waiting in the parking lot. He didn't spare him half a glance as he hurried inside. Tea or not, he was uneasy leaving her alone.

He unlocked his reception and crossed to his office. He unlocked his office and crossed to his cabinet. He took the silver key from his wallet and unlocked the cabinet. He emptied all the drawers into his briefcase. He took every sample he had. It would have to do. There was no burning hospital pharmacy he could raid this time around. He'd have to work with what he had and make up for what he didn't. He wasn't too concerned. Much could be accomplished with some creative operant conditioning.

His briefcase was filled to overflowing. He forced it shut. He took a moment to record a new voice message on his office phone, informing his patients that due to a family emergency his practice was temporarily closed. He wrote a similar message on a sheet of paper and taped it to the reception door. He gathered his briefcase, locked his office, and locked his reception up behind him as he left. His patient was waiting outside the door.

"Doc, what's—"

"Read the note," he said dismissively. "I'm sorry, I have to go."

He got in his car. He took out his cell phone. He opened the app and scrolled through the three cameras. The bedroom camera was off. The kitchen camera was off. The living room camera was on.

She wasn't there.

He closed the app. He put the cell phone away. He patted the briefcase on the seat beside him and turned the key. The engine rumbled.

He raced for home.

HE PULLED into the driveway. He seized his briefcase and got out of the car. He was halfway to the door when he heard "Ahoy!" He stopped, swore to himself, then turned around.

"Morning, neighbor!" Lou waved to him from his front yard.

"Good morning," he called in return. He started again toward the house but Lou put down his hedge trimmers and moseyed toward him. He cast a glance toward his house to ensure the blinds were drawn, then met Lou at the foot of his driveway. Lou shielded his eyes against the sun.

"Funny seeing you around this time of day," Lou said. "You run out of patients or what?" Lou slapped his knee and gave a hoot. "Then again, who's got the patience for all those patients, you know what I'm saying? Can't blame you, friend. Damn crazies."

"As a matter of fact, it's a family emergency," he said, and he couldn't keep the shortness out of his tone. Lou was immediately chastened.

"Ah, gee, I'm sorry to hear that. Family emergency, you say? Parents or something? I guess you'll be heading out of town then."

"I catch a flight this afternoon." He couldn't remember exactly what he'd told Snoopy Lou about his family, only that he had none in the area.

"Anything I can do while you're gone?" Lou asked. "Mow the lawn? Look in on the house, maybe?"

"It's all right," he said. "I've got it covered. And anyway, I shouldn't be gone long."

"I'm happy to help if you need me," Lou said. "Way I see it, I owe you, me and everybody else. All the work you do, keeping the crazies in check. If it wasn't for guys like you we'd be damn near overrun. Seems like they're popping up right and left these days, each one worse than the last. City really oughta build another hospital, at least to keep 'em all contained. They never did find out what caused that fire, did they? Damnedest thing."

He nodded vaguely.

Lou went on. "Me, I always thought it was that girl that escaped, but they said they was pretty sure it wasn't her. Point of origin or whatever it's called was in the cafeteria, and she was always kept in her room. Still, funny how she got out, ain't it? All those people dying in the halls while she's locked in her room, and somehow she escapes. I still wonder sometimes where she went." Lou laughed. "Bet there's a piece of work you're glad you never saw again, huh? What was it they called her condition?"

He hesitated. Lou raised an eyebrow. "Renfield syndrome," he answered at last. "Also known as clinical vampirism."

Lou shook his head. "Shoulda just called it what it is. Damn looney tunes. Boy, I still remember all the fuss about her in the papers. Boyfriend's mom found her feeding on her son's dead body. Drinking blood straight from his throat. If that's not murder I don't know what is. She got away with it too, pleading insanity. Claimed the boyfriend wanted her to do it. You ask me, they were both nuts. You'd have to be to get involved with someone like her."

He nodded vaguely. He looked toward the house.

Lou took the hint. "Guess I'd better let you get going, then. Give me a shout if you need something while you're gone. I'll be around."

"Thank you." He started up the driveway.

"I hope everything works out!" Lou called after him. He gripped his briefcase tighter.

"I'm sure it will," he called back. "It'll be all right." He muttered, "Everything's going to be fine."

HE UNLOCKED the door. He stepped inside. His heart was pounding and his skin was damp.

She was on the couch. Asleep. Just the way he'd left her.

He approached her warily.

She breathed deeply. She didn't move. He put his hand

on her shoulder and she didn't stir. He checked the bandage on her arm, then let her arm fall. It bounced off the couch twice before settling.

She was asleep.

He went upstairs. He went to the bedroom and into the closet. He found his shoe in the back and took out the key. He went downstairs and unlocked the basement door. He returned to the living room.

She hadn't moved.

He slid his arms beneath her, one at the shoulders and one at the knees. He picked her up. Her head sagged against his chest. He kissed her forehead and cradled her close. He descended slowly into the basement.

The basement was dark. It had no windows. It had no lights. He needed no light. He knew precisely where everything was. There wasn't much. There was a bed, with restraints for the head, arms, and legs. There was a tarp beneath the bed. There was a hose. And there was a muzzle, so she couldn't bite. So he wouldn't hear her screaming. It was everything he needed, all positioned on the far wall.

Which was why he was so surprised when he tripped.

The box, he thought, even as he fell. *I tripped over the box*. The box he'd filled with sharp objects and hidden down here for safekeeping. The box he'd pushed into the corner last night specifically so he wouldn't trip. It was right in his path at the base of the stairs. And as he stumbled over it, losing his balance, pitching forward, she came alive in his arms and scrambled out of them, just before he hit the floor. And as he hit the floor he saw her standing over him, the kitchen knife block raised above her head.

In the second it took for her to bring it down on him, he had two thoughts. The first was that the knife block was empty. He realized she had all the knives. And as the knife block crashed down and the dark basement became dark oblivion, his second thought was *oh shit*.

HE WOKE up.

It was dark. He was on his back. He was tied down at the wrists and ankles. He was naked.

He was not alone.

"Honey?" His voice croaked. He heard the fear in it. "Honey, let me go."

She didn't answer. He couldn't hear her. He could hear something. He could hear the clock.

Tik-tok. Tik-tok.

He struggled vainly against his bonds. He knew it was useless. He knew they would hold.

He'd chosen them himself.

A cold sweat broke out on his bare flesh. His breath echoed in the darkness. He heard the clock, *tik-tok*, *tik-tok*. The clock was in the room with him, it must be, to be so loud.

She was in the room too. He could feel her.

"Honey, please let me go."

She didn't respond. He turned his head side to side but couldn't see anything. He felt his chest heave. All he could hear was that damn clock.

Tik-tok. Tik-tok. Tik-tok.

When he felt it he nearly screamed, and all that stopped

him was the weight of it on his throat. The cold kiss of steel. He didn't breathe, he didn't dare breathe, not with the knife tucked under his chin. He felt the blade scrape over the stubble on his neck. He felt the point burrow into the hollow at its base.

He heard his voice. "Please don't, oh God, please don't." He felt the knife move higher. "Oh please God, please God, no."

The knife moved up his throat, then down. Up, then down. Now side to side. Up and down. Side to side. It came to rest in the hollow at the base of his neck. He was crying. Tears streamed and wouldn't stop.

"I love you," he begged. The knife trembled against his neck. "I only did it because I love you. Can't you see? I only wanted—".

He screamed as the knife pressed down and parted his skin. He could feel the tissue giving way, could feel the blood swell to the surface. It pooled in the hollow. It trickled down his chest. He felt her hands on her head, one on his forehead, one under his chin, and he whimpered as she tilted his head back. He felt her mouth on his throat, first her tongue, then her lips. She sucked slowly. She stroked his hair as she did.

"Oh dear God…"

The knife came again, this time on his chest. She cut a long stripe over his heart. He felt her weight on his hips as she straddled him, and she traced her mouth over the wound. Her tongue was rough. Her teeth scraped his skin. He let out a moan and she rocked her hips, and the knife opened him again.

She cut his cheek, cut a line from his ear to his mouth. She let his face bleed while she returned to his throat. He groaned. He shuddered beneath her. His skin was slick with sweat and blood. Her body slid on top of his. She was warm. She was familiar. She was naked. She sucked blood from the cut on his throat.

It was shallow, he realized, or else he would be bleeding out. If it was deep he would be losing consciousness. If it was deep the pain would be worse. There was pain, of course, but it wasn't that bad. It wasn't as bad as he'd thought. The worst part was the cut, that first splitting of skin, but after that the pain came from the air. It was cold in his basement. He'd made it that way. The cold air made the cuts sting, made them throb, made them raw, and the warmth of her mouth made it almost... better.

She made it better.

She cut him, but then she made it better.

It wasn't as bad as he'd thought.

She snaked up his body, bare skin on bare skin. She met his cheek with her tongue. She drank from the cut. She licked the length of it again and again. The cut was shallow. If it was deep he'd be bleeding out. He'd be losing consciousness. He'd be fading away.

He had never felt so alive.

She licked the length of the cut. She paused at his ear. She hummed contentedly. She nibbled the lobe. She swept her tongue across the cut and came to rest at his mouth. She licked his lips and he parted them for her.

Sweet, wet heat filled his mouth, tinged with salt, tinged with copper. Her kiss was bruising. Her skin was hot. He strained at his restraints, not to escape but to take her, to draw her closer, but they held, and he couldn't move. His hips writhed of their own accord and she matched him, she worsened his need. He panted. He moaned. He begged her, "Please."

She ground against him and whispered, "What?"

"Please. I need you. Oh God…"

"There's no God," she said. "Only me."

"Please. I need you. Oh Christ. Oh dear God—"

He felt the knife on his skin again, felt it skim along his jaw. It pricked beneath his chin. He whimpered. His hips bucked.

She said, "You love me."

"Oh yes. Oh God, yes."

"Say it."

"I love you, I love you, I—"

"Prove it."

The knife pricked beneath his chin. He didn't hesitate. He leaned into it, raising his chin. The knife slid in and blood seeped out. He took the blade deeper. He felt blood spill down his throat.

The knife vanished and her mouth replaced it. He closed his eyes and let her drink. When her lips found his he kissed her desperately. When she took him in he cried out in relief.

He laid still on the bed, arms gone numb, legs gone heavy. He heard his breathing and the sound of her mouth. She still drank. He heard the clock. *Tik-tok*. *Tik-tok*.

"Oh God," he groaned, "oh dear God…"

He turned his head but she followed, her teeth at his throat. He tugged on his restraints but it was no use.

Wretched tears flowed down his cheeks.

She lapped them up.

"It's all right," she said, and she kissed him sweetly. "You'll be fine," she said, and she laid her head on his chest. "You love me, don't you? You've loved me all along." She brought her mouth to his ear and whispered, "Now it's my turn to love you."

She kissed him. He whimpered. He heard the clock. *Tik-tok. Tik-tok.*

Tik. Tok.

Tik.

Tok.

For more of Jay Allisan's writing and updates on her
next book, visit www.jayallisan.com